BITTERSWEET MURDER

HAWG HEAVEN COZY MYSTERIES, BOOK 7

SUMMER PRESCOTT

SUMMER PRESCOTT BOOKS PUBLISHING

ACKNOWLEDGMENTS

As with so many things in life, sometimes it takes a village to write a book. Last month, when Summer Prescott Books Publishing hit a milestone of "likes" on our Facebook page, we held contests as part of our online celebration party. Some of the questions that we asked our beloved readers included:

What character would you like to see added to the Hawg Heaven series?

And of course, the delicious:

What foods would you like to see featured in the Hawg Heaven series?

The character that I came up with was inspired by an

idea from Cindy Gifford, and was a much-needed addition to the Hawg Heaven cast. Thank you so much, Cindy!! Shelly is a character who provides just the comic relief that we need in this sometimes very sobering series. We do tackle some heavy issues in here, but we love the laughter that balances it out.

The recipe suggestion which inspired the entire plot for the book came from Joanne Kocourek, who might be a bit surprised at how her idea was used, and the mouthwatering idea for the cover of the book came from Lesley Spicer. I seriously had to eat brownies and bacon while writing this book – way to go Joanne and Lesley!!

I seriously couldn't do what I do without the incredible support from readers – you all rock!! Thanks so much for not only reading the books, but participating in events and providing valuable feedback!!!

Hugs and sunshine,

Summer

CHAPTER 1

"ROSSIE, honey, maybe you need a vacation. Either close up Hawg Heaven for a few days, or let José be in charge while you take some time for yourself," Rossalyn Channing's mother, Margo, suggested.

Rossalyn Channing's hands were wrapped around her mug of coffee as she sat at her parent's kitchen table; she drew warmth from it, despite the very pleasant temperature of a late summer in northern Illinois. Her head bowed as she stared into her cup, her dark hair forming a protective curtain around her.

"If I'm not working, I have too much time to think," she sighed.

Her husband, who had been declared KIA by the military, had recently resurfaced, nearly a year after she'd buried his empty casket. His reappearance had rocked her world and left her feeling betrayed; he hadn't come home immediately upon his release, but had instead been trying for months to become accustomed to normal civilian life.

In his absence, Rossie had continued to raise their thirteen-year-old son, and had opened a café just a couple of hours south of her parents' house. She'd cried and grieved and had carried on with her life, as a military wife is supposed to do, but Will Channing's reappearance alive and well had startled her badly. She didn't know how to handle it, and was filled with conflicted feelings. Will had gone to Florida with another Marine vet to give her time to think, but all she wanted to do now was to avoid thinking.

Margo gazed at her daughter helplessly, her heart breaking. "What can I do?" she asked simply.

Rossie shook her head, a single tear streaking its way down her cheek. "This is just like anything else, Mom. I have to tough it out on my own. I'll figure things out. It's just going to take some time."

"You always do," her mother nodded, reaching

across the table to take her hand. "But how would you feel about your father and I taking Ryan for a couple of weeks? We're going to head out to California for a bit. We found an adorable little cottage on the beach that we're going to rent, and were thinking that Ryan might like to spend some time working on his tan."

Rossalyn nodded. "It'd probably be good for him to have a change of scenery. Did you mention it to him?"

"Well, I didn't. I wanted to talk to you first, but he's been keeping your father company in the garage so…" Margo smiled.

As if on cue, the door from the garage burst open and Ryan came flying in.

"Hey Mom! Can I go to California?" he asked, his eyes brighter than she'd seen them since his dad left for Florida.

"Who'll take care of Barney?" Rossie asked, trying not to smile at Ryan's exuberance.

He loved his newly adopted hound dog more than life itself, and she'd put money on the belief that he hadn't considered having to leave his canine friend behind.

Ryan frowned. "Well… he's a good boy. He'd be company for you and keep you safe while I'm gone," he replied earnestly.

Rossie couldn't help herself, she grinned. "You've thought all of this through, haven't you?"

"It's been a long time since I swam in the ocean."

"What's in it for me?" Rossalyn teased, knowing that she was going to let him go.

"Umm… I don't know. Personal time? You can drink wine and take baths and all that girlie stuff without having to worry about hanging out with me," he shrugged.

"But I like hanging out with you."

"Then you'll be really excited when I get back. C'mon Mom, Grandpa really wants me to go. I'll bring you a seashell or something."

"Well, I suppose if Grandpa really wants you to go…"

"He does," Ryan nodded, sneaking two cookies from a plate on the counter.

"Then go tell him you'll be his California buddy," Rossie smiled, finally letting him off the hook.

"Yes!" he took off for the garage, where Rossalyn's dad was puttering so that he'd be out of the line of fire after spilling the beans about the trip. "Thanks, Mom!"

"You're welcome," Rossie called after him, her smile fading a bit as he disappeared into the garage.

"You need this time to yourself," Margo studied her daughter. "Make the most of it."

"At this point, I don't even know what that means."

"Sometimes our answers come to us when we're not looking for them."

"You mean I should just carry on and see what happens?"

"That usually works for you. You figure things out while you're busy living life. So do that. Go live life and try not to worry for a while. Even in California, I'm just a phone call away."

"You're the best, Mom. Thank you," Rossalyn's smile was faint, but grateful.

CHAPTER 2

Rossie's cozy house felt unnaturally still and empty with Ryan gone, and she was actually glad that she had Barney to keep her company. Rather than leaving the mellow hound home alone during the day, she took him to work with her, where he happily snoozed his day away on the back patio. Business had been booming. The town of Chatsworth sat at the convergence of three major highways, and Hawg Heaven was one of the first businesses that hungry travelers saw when exiting from any of them. She had a regular crowd from town as well, and was facing the fact that she was going to need to expand, sooner rather than later.

Rossalyn had been in her office all morning, letting

her crew handle the breakfast rush, while she looked at expansion bids from various contractors.

"Whew, this is going to be expensive," she sighed, shaking her head at the figures running across the pages.

"If you need someone to talk to, there are plenty of customers out here," Ashley Martin had clearly heard Rossalyn's murmurings before she poked her head in the office door, her long blond ringlets barely contained in a massive bun at the nape of her neck.

"Do you need help?" Rossie started to rise.

"No, ma'am, I'm just messing with you," Ashley giggled, her sunny presence always a welcome distraction. "José was just wanting to check with you on the lunch special and make sure that you approved."

"Are there samples?" Rossie's stomach suddenly gurgled with longing. She hadn't eaten since lunch yesterday, and her body was finally reminding her about it.

"Yes, ma'am. They're fresh. I thought you might

want to come to the kitchen for a tasting and refresh your coffee. I just made a fresh pot."

Rossie's stomach growled even louder.

"Well, I guess that's my answer," Ashley grinned. "I'll go fix you a plate," she reached for her boss's nearly empty coffee cup and headed for the door.

"I'll be right there, Ash. Thanks," Rossie called after her.

She walked through the dining area on her way to the kitchen, greeting the locals by name and making sure that she checked to see that all the unfamiliar faces were happy too.

"Whatever magic you're making smells amazing," Rossalyn smiled at José when she walked into the kitchen. He spun his spatula in his signature move and reached for a luscious-looking plate of food, handing it to her with a mock bow.

"Wow, this looks great… what are those?" she asked, pointing to some bite-sized tidbits.

"Loco mac and cheese bites," he announced proudly. "It's mac and cheese with bacon and fresh jalapeno, dipped in a light cornmeal batter and deep-fried."

"They're seriously the best thing ever," Ashley chimed in gazing at José with admiration for more than the food. "I think I've gained ten pounds today because of those little flavor bombs," she shook her head.

"Oh my, that sounds decadent. Tell me about the pulled pork and greens," she checked out her plate, her mouth watering.

"The pulled pork has a bourbon barbeque sauce, with just a little kick, and the mustard greens are whipped with cream cheese and spices."

Rossalyn loved that José was an inventive and skilled cook, and was thankful that she had a fast metabolism.

"Oh wow, you've outdone yourself this time," she enthused after sampling one of the bites.

"Glad you like it," José beamed and went back to putting a dry rub on a brisket.

Rossalyn glanced at the prep area in the back and noticed that something, or more to the point, some-one, was missing.

"Where's Garrett?" she asked, putting a hand in front of her mouth because she was still chewing.

José and Ashley exchanged a glance.

"He's going to be late," Ashley spoke up. "He had some kind of argument with his crazy landlady or something."

Rossie nodded, then swallowed before speaking. "Poor guy. I hope that he can move out of the boardinghouse soon. It's not necessarily the greatest environment for a young man just starting out."

"I think he's saving up for an apartment," José commented, absorbed in his task, but paying attention to the conversation as well. The clever young man missed nothing.

"Hmm... well, maybe I can give him an advance or..." Rossie began, thinking.

José shook his head. "Nope, he won't take it. I already tried to help him, but he wants to make it on his own."

"Well, that's admirable, and something that I totally understand," Rossalyn had a faraway look in her eyes, but snapped out of it. "José, you're going to be a big hit with this special. Great job," she raised her fork in tribute and headed back to the office, only to nearly run into a tall, curvaceous woman around her own age.

"Oh, excuse me," Rossie said, lifting her plate so that it didn't spill down the front of the woman's navy blue polo and work pants. "There usually isn't anyone down here, so I just came barging through. Can I help you with something?" she smiled.

"I'm the oldest of four siblings, don't worry, I'm used to dodging food, and if it's as good as it smells, I'm certainly not above catching it on the way down and eating it," the woman grinned. "Are you the manager or the owner here?"

That was a question that always gave Rossalyn a bit of a start, because it meant that whomever was asking was there either in an official capacity, or to complain, and she dreaded the complaints.

"I'm Rossalyn Channing, the owner. What can I do for you?" she asked, feeling awkward about standing there with a plate of food.

"Well, I didn't mean to interrupt your brunch. I'm

Shelly Stroud, Fire Inspector, and I'm here to do a routine safety audit."

"Oh, no worries. What do you need from me?"

"Not a thing," Shelly answered, pulling a small clipboard out of a cargo pocket in her pants. "I'll just need to take a look around and make sure that all of your detection devices are operational and that you don't have risk factors for fires. It can be tough for restaurants sometimes. So, after I do my inspection, I'll draw up a report and get one copy to you and a copy to the city."

"Oh, okay," Rossie nodded. "I'll be back here in my office if you need anything."

"Sounds good, thanks," Shelly gave her a brief smile and headed toward the kitchen.

"You know, that food isn't going to do you any good unless you pick up the fork," Shelly remarked, knocking lightly on the door of Rossie's office to get her attention.

"Oh, I'm sorry," Rossalyn shook her head a bit, hoping to clear it. "Was everything okay?"

"Yup. You passed with flying colors." Shelly paused for a moment, regarding the woman in front of her carefully. "I'm just one of those rude, brash types who says exactly what she thinks, so you'll have to forgive me, but... you look like you're having a rough day," she observed, leaning against the doorframe and crossing her arms.

Too beaten down to put up a front, and feeling strangely comfortable around this total stranger, Rossie nodded. "Rough few weeks actually." She gestured to the chair across from her and Shelly plopped into it, the leather creaking under her weight.

"Business bad?"

"No, business is great. It's me who's a mess," Rossie admitted.

"This isn't one of those middle-of-nowhere towns where you're shunned if you haven't lived here your whole life, is it?" Shelly's eyebrows rose.

"No, people here have been really nice. Are you new in town?"

"Yup, just relocated to join the fire department. I'm the only woman over there. It's been interesting," she rolled her eyes.

"I can't even imagine."

"I'll just be honest with you, I've been bored to death since I moved here. You wouldn't want to get together for a movie or something tonight, would you? It might be good for both of us," Shelly invited.

On a rare impulse, Rossalyn accepted. "Yeah, that sounds pretty great, actually. I haven't just hung out with a friend for ages. Is there anything good playing?"

"I don't know… do you like kung fu?" Shelly's grin was mischievous.

CHAPTER 3

Rossalyn carried what was left of a bucket of popcorn, and wiped her eyes as she and Shelly came out of the darkened movie theater into the lobby.

"Oh my gosh, I don't think I've laughed that hard in a long time," she gasped.

"Right?" Shelly agreed, grinning from ear to ear. "I hoped that it wasn't going to be lame, but I never expected it to be that good. Romantic comedies can go either way."

"The part where they went to the wine cellar… and the spider…" Rossie burst into giggles, grabbing onto Shelly's arm for support as the two wove their way out the door, laughing together.

"Well, fancy meetin' you here," a smoke-roughened female voice called out from beside the ticket booth.

Rossalyn turned to see Eliza Bouchard, who ran the boardinghouse where Garrett, her assistant cook lived, smoking a cigarette and leaning against the building.

"Oh, hi," she said, instantly sobering.

"Yeah, great to see you too," Eliza drawled sarcastically, then turned her attention to Shelly. "You her bodyguard?"

"Only on Thursdays," was the deadpan answer. That threw Eliza off a bit, and to recover, she tossed her cigarette on the sidewalk and ground it out with her well-worn purple flip-flop.

"Been meanin' to talk to you," Eliza rasped, turning her attention back to Rossalyn and missing the satisfied smirk on Shelly's face.

"Oh?"

"Yeah. Garrett's been workin' for you for quite a while now, and he lives over at my place," she began, and Rossie wondered where Eliza was going.

"Yes, I know."

"I'm having a family reunion next week, and I want to do a hog roast. I figure since me and Garrett are practically family, that should earn me some kinda discount or something," she crossed her arms over her bony chest and stared at Rossie, daring her to disagree.

"Oh, well, I… actually don't do hog roasts. I wouldn't even know where to begin."

"Oh please. Don't tell me that your Mexican boy don't know how to roast a hog. That kid could cook a pile of dirt and make it taste good. Just let him watch some cookin' videos on his phone and he could do it in a heartbeat," Eliza clearly wasn't in the mood to take no for an answer.

Rossalyn winced when she called José 'your Mexican boy,' but tried not to react. Shelly was digging into her box of chocolate-covered raisins and popping them in her mouth, watching the two other women like it was a tennis match.

"Well, this is really short notice, and I don't think I have the staff to cater an event while we're open for business…" Rossie floundered, spitting out every excuse that she could think of.

"Oh, you're too good to take my money? Yeah, I heard that you were snooty like that," Eliza made a face.

"Lemme get this straight," Shelly dove in, looking like she relished the opportunity. "You want her to completely rearrange her schedule to staff an event that you want her to give you a discount on, and then you think that you'll get your way by insulting her?" she challenged.

"What business is it of yours? Who are you anyway? I ain't seen you around here before, and I know everybody. You one of those lesbians from the city?" Eliza's eyes narrowed at her new target.

Rossie let out an astonished gasp and Shelly cracked up.

"Why, you looking for a girlfriend, honey?" she asked, batting her eyes.

"You just keep away from me," Eliza warned. "And you," she turned back to Rossie. "You gonna do a hog roast or not? I'd hate to have to ask Garrett to find a new place," she threatened.

"That's shameful," Rossie's mouth dropped open. "You'd toss Garrett out if I don't agree to your stupid hog roast?"

"Life's full of choices, sugarbritches," Eliza's mouth cracked into a nasty grin.

Shelly stepped forward. "And you're full of…" she began, but Rossie put a hand up to stop her.

"I'll do it," she blurted. "I'll work up pricing this evening, and you can come into the café to go over the details with me tomorrow," Rossie's jaw was set.

"See… ain't it nice how things can work out between neighbors," Eliza smirked.

"I wonder if your detectors are up to code," Shelly mused, an eyebrow raised at the tiny wisp of a woman in front of her.

"I don't like you," Eliza commented, giving Shelly another once-over.

"I get that a lot," the firefighter smiled.

Not quite knowing how to take the much larger and

infinitely wittier woman, Eliza turned and started walking away.

"Hey," Shelly barked, making Eliza jump. She turned around and shot a glare at her.

"What?"

Shelly bent down, picked up the smashed cigarette butt and tossed it at Eliza. "You forgot this. There are fines for littering in this town. Keep Chatsworth clean," she grinned.

Startled at the unexpected action, Eliza caught and held the butt in her hand, mouth open, as Rossie took Shelly's arm and steered her away.

CHAPTER 4

ROSSIE STOOD, arms crossed, staring at the growing hole that José and Garrett were digging behind the boardinghouse.

"You guys, I'm really sorry about this. This is above and beyond the call of duty," she worried, hating making them do the labor necessary to roast an entire pig luau style.

Eliza had insisted on a 150-pound pig, so the hole had to be immense, and just cooking the beast would take twelve to fourteen hours after the extensive prep was done. Rossie had no idea that roasting a whole pig was so labor intensive, but José and Garrett both had seemed enthusiastic about the idea, thankfully.

Tomorrow, during the family reunion that Eliza had planned, Garrett and Rossie would be at the boarding-house, catering the event, while Ashley and José handled the crowd at Hawg Heaven. Once the whole pig had been lifted out of the ground, with the help of four of Eliza's relatives, Rossie and Garrett would bring out the massive pans of side dishes, cornbread, and desserts, while the cantankerous hostess supplied iced tea, lemonade, and multiple kegs of cheap beer. It was definitely not a day that Rossie was looking forward to, and she really hoped that José's method of cooking the pig would have the desired turnout.

"That hole don't look big enough," Eliza groused, peering down into it.

While Rossalyn entertained dark thoughts about pushing her into it, Shelly, of course, had a comeback ready.

"Is that what your vast amount of experience in culinary arts tells you?" she asked sweetly.

"Art... what? I don't do none of that voodoo stuff. Why are you here anyway?" Eliza shot back.

Shelly tapped the logo on her shirt. "Fire Department," she said slowly and loudly. "When they light this sucker up, there has to be an observer out here, since it's within town limits."

"Firefighter, huh? I knew you were a lesbian. Don't you be giving me any funny looks, ya hear?" Eliza shook at finger at Shelly and kept her distance.

Rossie had to turn away and stifle her laugh. Hanging out with Shelly had been good for her. She was a great listener, and the two of them were already comfortable with each other, having shared a lot of laughs. Shelly seemed to be the person who would say what everyone else was thinking, much to Rossie's shock and delight.

The hole got deeper and wider, and just after sunset, they were ready to light the fire that would heat the bed of rocks in the bottom of the pit. Once the flames had died down and produced coals, the pig would be placed in the pit, and buried, ready to eat around dinner time the next day. It was late when the last bit of earth was tamped down over the whole animal. Rossie hadn't been able to bring herself to watch when they lowered the pig down into the earth. The image of her husband's casket was still too fresh in her mind.

"Well, that was more fun than I've had in a while," Shelly commented dryly, as Garrett went inside to his room and José headed home. "You look pretty beat too, kiddo. Wine and pizza at your house?"

"I believe you read my mind," Rossie gave her a weary smile.

With Barney the hound between their feet, Rossie and Shelly chowed down on pepperoni pizza and chased it with red wine, talking like old friends.

"So, what on earth brought someone with your qualifications to Chatsworth, Illinois?" Rossie asked, nibbling on a crust.

"Sexual harassment," was the nonchalant, but vaguely sad, reply.

Rossie set down her wine glass and pizza crust. "What?"

"I was rising quickly through the ranks in Detroit. The top guy told me I'd rise even faster if I came over to his house a couple times a week. I told him what he could do with his offer, and he told me to leave the department or he'd fire me. Since he wanted to ruin my career, and my life, he also said that if I applied to any major departments, like Chicago, New York, the places where I could really make a difference, he'd make sure that I never got hired. My only hope for survival was to find a middle-of-nowhere backwater and just disappear. So here I am," Shelly's tone turned the slightest bit bitter and she finished her wine, holding up her glass for more.

"Oh, that's awful," Rossie's forehead creased with anger and she shook her head. "Couldn't you go to the police or something? Or sue?"

"Nope, they were all in the same league. The guys supported each other, and I was the odd woman out. I'd have gotten nowhere in the courts there, so I just went on my way."

"So, how did you happen to choose Chatsworth?"

"I printed the page of open positions, cut them apart and put them in a hat, and literally shook them up, closed my eyes and picked one."

"Didn't you have any friends or family in the area? Wasn't it hard to just… leave?"

"My parents are in a retirement community in Florida. I go to see them every few months. I worked so hard all the time that I didn't have time to make friends. I was married to the job, as they say."

"That must've been hard for a social person like you."

"Yes and no. I missed not having anyone to talk to, but I kept myself so busy that I didn't really have time to think about it very often," Shelly shrugged.

"So, I'm guessing that you're changing your approach to life now?" Rossie asked softly.

"Yep. I'm gonna eat, drink, and be merry. I'll hang out with friends and take time to smell the roses. I worked my tail off for years, and all I've got to show for it is a nice retirement. Something tells me that there's more to life than that, and I'm determined to find out," she raised her glass and Rossie clinked hers against it.

"Well, good for you," she smiled. "And good for me."

CHAPTER 5

MEETING ELIZA'S brothers and boyfriend had Rossalyn wondering how the woman was so darn irascible. The men were polite, jovial, and more than ready to lend a helping hand. Mort, her older brother, had a red beard and reminded Rossie of a happy leprechaun. Sid, her younger brother, was thin, with a receding hairline and a ready smile; and Chuck, her on-again-off-again boyfriend, had a hearty laugh and a full head of wavy, salt-and-pepper hair. He was handsome in his own way, and Rossie couldn't figure out what he saw in cranky Eliza.

The men all grabbed shovels, with Garrett joining them, and began carefully removing dirt that was about a foot deep on top of the pig. Once the dirt was gone, the four men each took a corner, and grabbed the edges of the chicken wire that had been placed under the pig to help lift it, intact, from the hole, while it was still covered in protective cloths and burlap.

"Something don't smell right," Mort wrinkled his nose.

"That Mexican kid is gonna be sorry if he messed up my pig," Eliza thundered.

"Oh, hold your britches, lil girl," Mort admonished, drawing a scathing look from his sister. "You can't really tell how it came out until you get the sacks off."

While Rossie appreciated the fact that Mort had just verbally smacked down his obnoxious sister, she had to agree that the smell coming from the pit was definitely not appetizing.

"Well, then, quit messin' around. Get it up out of the hole and take the sacks off, so we can see it."

A crowd of family that looked to be about a hundred strong, gathered around the hole, many of them fanning the air in front of themselves or holding their noses. Rossie and Garrett exchanged a nervous look, both hoping that the expensive pig had turned out well. The four men lifted the chicken wire, encased with burlap and special cloth, and set it on a large picnic table beside the hole.

"Hmm… ain't never seen one that hung over the sides like that," Sid grunted, setting his corner down and pointing out that the bundle was indeed longer than the picnic table.

"That must be one heckuva huge pig," Chuck agreed, setting down his corner.

"Well, let's take a look at it," Eliza nudged Mort, who began peeling the special cloth and burlap sacks back, layer by layer.

The crowd, which had been talking and laughing while watching the unveiling of their dinner, became deathly quiet, when the shape that began to emerge from beneath the layers of cloth became very un-piglike. There were whispers, and murmurs, then a collective gasp as the final cloth was peeled back to reveal a very well-cooked middle-aged man. Women screamed and drew their children away. Some of the folks who were closest ran away gagging, their eyes filled with horror.

"Couldn't have happened to a nicer guy," Mort said, making eye contact with Eliza, who just stood, stone faced, nodding.

Rossie couldn't take her eyes away from the lump on the table. "How could this have happened," she whispered. "It's impossible... I saw them put the pig in. I watched the whole time."

"I'll call José and let him know that he and Ashley will be closing without us tonight," Garrett said quietly, pulling out his phone and walking away from the corpse.

Someone else called 911, and first responders, including Shelly, arrived. As a matter of protocol, the ambulance and fire truck stayed until Officer Morgan Tyler arrived, followed closely by the coroner and a forensics team. Relatives huddled together away from the horrific sight beside the pit, some sobbing softly, others just staring into space, pale and wan beneath their burnished summer skin. The entire lot surrounding the boardinghouse was cordoned off with crime scene tape, and no one was allowed to leave without giving a statement. Shelly came by to give Rossie's shoulder a reassuring squeeze before heading to her rig.

Rossie and Garrett sat on the front porch of the boardinghouse for a long time, waiting to be interviewed by the police; when Hawg Heaven closed for the night, José came over to wait with them, knowing that as one of the cooks who prepared the pig, the police would probably want to talk to him too.

There were more than a dozen police officers on the scene, but Morgan Tyler came over to interview Rossie and her employees personally, joining them on the porch, away from Eliza's stunned family members.

"Rossalyn, Garrett, José," he greeted each of them. "This shouldn't take too long. The only reason we had to keep you here is because you were involved in the events leading up to… what happened. Did any of you recognize the victim?"

Rossie and José both shook their head, but surprisingly, Garrett nodded and said, "Yes sir, I recognized him. It was Miss Eliza's ex-husband."

"Yes it was. How did you know him?" Morgan's focus was solely on Garrett now.

"He came by the boardinghouse a couple of times. Every time he did, they'd fight." Beads of sweat popped out on the slightly overweight young man's upper lip under the policeman's intense scrutiny. Garrett was very much a blend-into-the-background kind of guy.

"What would they fight about?"

"Lots of stuff. Money, their divorce, a bunch of things. I tried not to listen, but they yelled pretty loud and it came up through the vents in my floor because my room is on the second floor," he explained earnestly, flicking his overly long blond hair out of his eyes.

"When was the last time that this happened?"

"Yesterday morning. I didn't have to be at work until noon, so I heard them again."

"Yesterday," Morgan's eyebrows rose. "Did you happen to hear what they were arguing about?"

"Yes sir," Garrett nodded. "He wanted to come to the family reunion. Said that he was family too, cuz they'd been married. She said no way, and told him to leave lots of times, but I guess he wasn't leaving until he had his say. They both made threats. He told her that she better be decent to him when he showed up, and she told him that if he showed his face he'd be leaving…" Garrett swallowed hard and looked very uncomfortable.

"Go on," Morgan prompted.

"That he'd be leaving in a body bag," the young man finished quietly.

Rossie and José looked at each other in shock.

"They were still at it when I got in the shower to get ready for work, but they were both gone by the time I got out."

"I see," Morgan nodded, then seemed to remember that Rossalyn and José were still there. "Do either of you two have anything to add that might aid in the investigation?"

Both shook their head and said no.

"Okay then. We'll probably have more questions for you once we investigate the scene, but we're done here for now. Thanks for your cooperation."

When Officer Tyler left, Garrett turned to José. "Hey man, can I crash on your couch tonight? I really don't want to be here right now."

"Of course," José nodded. "Let's go."

The two left, and Rossie headed toward her car, checking her phone for messages. There was only one text, from Shelly: *Wow, who was the hot cop at the hog roast???*

Despite the events of the day, that made her smile.

CHAPTER 6

ELIZA BOUCHARD STOOD in front of the register at Hawg Heaven, hands on hips, tapping her foot.

"I want my money back, every dime," she announced loudly, drawing startled looks from a handful of travelers who were eating, and a series of eyerolls from locals who would expect nothing less from the notorious firebrand.

Rossalyn was trying very hard to maintain a neutral expression and professional demeanor, and gave the tiny despot a tight smile.

"Eliza, this is neither the time nor the place to discuss such things. Now, I know you've been through a difficult…"

"Don't you try to change the subject," she bellowed in her raspy smoker's voice. "You just stick your grubby hand right inside that cash register right now and give me my money back. I paid for a hog roast and I didn't get one."

"Ashley, can you take over here so that I can go speak with Ms. Bouchard privately?" Rossie snagged the young woman on her way by.

"Oh no, you don't. I ain't going nowhere to talk about nothing. I want my money back and I want it now," Eliza yelled.

A couple of diners put money on their tables and hurried out, which infuriated Rossie. It was time to pull the gloves off. She was about a head taller than Eliza Bouchard, and when she stepped from behind the register, she towered over the bristling little woman. Rossie stepped squarely into the woman's personal space and inclined her head so that only Eliza could hear her.

"Now you listen to me, Eliza Bouchard," she growled, somehow managing to keep a deceptively pleasant look on her face for the customers who were watching. "You are in here disturbing my customers and making a scene and I won't have it. You either march yourself out the door right now, or I swear to all that's holy, I'll throw you over my shoulder and toss you out."

Eliza opened her mouth to speak, saw the look in Rossie's eyes, and changed her mind. Her eyes narrowed.

"You threatening me, Miss Priss?" she challenged, her voice much quieter.

"I don't make threats, Eliza," Rossie stared her down. "Turn around and leave. Now."

Defiant, Eliza suddenly swept her arm across the counter in front of the register, dumping a container of toothpicks, a jar of change for the homeless, and a stand with various candy and gum products onto the floor. Rossie was on her in a flash, pinning her arms behind her and shoving her toward the front door before the tiny woman even knew what was happening.

"Call the police, Ash. I'll be out front," Rossie called out over her shoulder, while propelling a squalling, kicking, and snarling Eliza outside.

Morgan Tyler took Rossie's report while another patrol car took Eliza to jail for disturbing the peace.

"Pretty impressive that you subdued her until we arrived," Morgan smiled. "Where'd you learn those ninja moves?"

"With the nature of my husband's work, I was alone quite a bit," she shrugged. "I took some classes in self-defense."

"I heard about your husband coming back, that's great news," his smile was forced this time. Morgan had tried on multiple occasions to get Rossie to date him.

"Wow, this is a small town," was her unsmiling comment.

Morgan was saved from commenting by Shelly's arrival.

"Hey girlfriend, I heard there was a ruckus down here, and I had to come check it out," she grinned, glancing from Rossie to Morgan and back again, either oblivious or unconcerned about the tension between the two. "I don't believe we've met," she held her hand out to Morgan. "Shelly Stroud."

Morgan shook her hand and introduced himself. "You must be the new firefighter I heard about."

Shelly turned to Rossie. "See, that's what's so great about our boys in blue, they're so observant," she teased, tapping the logo on her polo shirt.

"Welcome to Chatsworth," Morgan chuckled. "And my apologies in advance. It can't be easy being the only female in the department, and one that outranks most of the team."

"I'm tough, I can handle it, but thanks."

"No problem. I'm going to be taking a statement from Rossalyn now, but it was nice to meet you," he dismissed her kindly.

"You too. I'll be inside mowing through one of José's sandwiches if you're hungry after your interrogation," she grinned. "See ya inside, Ross," she squeezed her friend's arm on her way by.

"Interesting character," Morgan observed, when Shelly was out of earshot.

Rossie walked him through what had happened with Eliza in a matter of minutes, and he snapped his notebook shut when they were finished.

"You want to press charges?" he asked.

"I have no idea," Rossie sighed. "I know she's going through a tough time, so I don't want to add fuel to that fire, but I don't want her to think she can come in here shouting up the place either."

"Well, you've actually done us a bit of a favor, no matter which way you go. She's one of the suspects in the hog roast murder, and she's in our custody now. Maybe being in jail will help her to come clean, if she actually did it."

"Scared straight? Doesn't seem likely with Eliza Bouchard," Rossalyn made a face.

"She's a horse of a very peculiar color," Morgan agreed, nodding.

"How long do I have to make up my mind about pressing charges?"

"Twenty-four hours. If we don't hear from you by this time tomorrow, she walks."

"Well, I won't make up my mind for a bit, that'll buy you some time."

"I appreciate it," Morgan touched the brim of his hat. "Mind if I come in and have a sandwich?"

"Help yourself, José is cooking up a storm," Rossie smiled, knowing how pleased Shelly would be to see the handsome cop walking in.

CHAPTER 7

MORGAN TYLER WAS TRYING HARD NOT to lose patience with Eliza Bouchard. She stubbornly refused to answer questions, repeatedly asked if she could bum a cigarette from one of the officers, and had a litany of complaints. One would've thought that he was the suspect, being subjected to enhanced interrogation.

"Now Eliza," he tried again. "If you'll cooperate with me just a little bit, it'll help me find your ex-husband's killer that much quicker."

"Why, so you can give him a medal? That fool deserved what he got, why should I want to punish someone for doing what shoulda been done a long time ago?" she crossed her arms defiantly.

"When you say things like that, it makes me think that I ought to be taking a closer look at you as the perpetrator," Morgan's voice was mild, but his implication was clear.

"You think I did this? Pish…" Eliza made a disgusted sound. "Honey, if I was gonna do the old man in, I'd have done it a long time ago. Like maybe when he was beating me with a tire iron because I didn't get dinner on the table fast enough. I'd love to take credit for it, but no, handsome, somebody got to him before I could."

"Any idea who?" the officer's tone was more subdued. Eliza's matter-of-fact retelling of the abuse she'd endured at the hands of the victim elicited a compassionate response, even though he was still considering the possibility that the woman in front of him had murdered her ex.

"There's a long line of folks who wouldn't mind seeing him dead, I'll tell you that. Kinda hard to narrow it down," Eliza shook her head.

"So, a lot of folks wouldn't mind seeing him dead, but who might be motivated enough to actually make it happen?"

"Ain't that your job to find out?" she challenged.

"That's why I'm here talking to you," he levelled her with a glance.

Eliza looked away, and it appeared to Morgan that she was hiding something.

"Can't help you," she muttered.

Morgan nodded, seeing that he wasn't going to get any further. "Fine. You go back to your cell and think about it some more," he stood and motioned to the officer in the back of the room to take her away.

"I wanna go home, I told you that already. How long you plannin' on holdin' me here? I got rights ya know."

"Your charges are pending. We can't let you go until we see if they're dropped or not," Morgan shrugged. He'd like nothing better than to have her never-ceasing, raspy bellow out of the building, but he also had a feeling that she knew more than she was saying, and his best guess was that she was protecting someone.

Mort Bouchard had a frown on his face as he sat across the table from Officer Morgan Tyler.

"Why do we have to go through this again? I told ya everythin' that I knew when you asked me the first time," the burly redhead insisted.

"The more questions we ask, the better chance that you might recall some details which might help me to catch the killer," Morgan explained, thinking that stubbornness clearly ran in the Bouchard family, though Mort was far more genial than his sister had been.

"Seems to me that he did the rest of us a favor," Mort grumbled.

"Homicide is against the law, Mort," Morgan reminded him.

"Yeah, so what do you wanna know?"

"Have you ever had any altercations with the victim?"

"Oh, heck, yeah. When he was married to Eliza, I told him off more than once. Told him if he ever laid hands on her again, he'd have to answer to me."

"When was the last time you had an interaction with him?"

Mort stroked his beard for a moment, thinking. "Gotta say it was… right before they got divorced. I let him know that I knew he didn't care about the restraining order. That piece of paper meant nothing to him. I made it clear that if he came around my sister, it'd be the last thing he ever did."

"You do know how incriminating that sounds, right?"

"I don't know nothing about that, I'm just tellin' you how it went down."

Morgan blinked for a moment, then continued.

"Were you aware that he planned to attend your family reunion?"

"Yeah, Eliza said somethin' about it, and me and Sid told her that we'd handle it if he showed up."

"What did you mean when you said you'd handle it," Morgan leaned forward.

"That we'd throw him out, and if he raised a ruckus, we'd make sure he stayed out."

"And how would you accomplish that?" Morgan

asked casually, wondering if he was about to hear a confession to murder.

Mort shrugged. "We'd just give him a beatdown. Let him spend the family reunion in the hospital."

"So you literally planned to use violence?"

"If he came in and started actin' the fool, yeah, we were gonna do whatever we had to do to shut him down."

"Including murder?"

Mort rolled his eyes. "Whaddya think I'm stupid or something? I'm not gonna waste my life rottin' in jail for the likes of that pile of garbage. Heck no, we wasn't gonna kill nobody. We was just gonna teach him a little lesson," he smirked.

"And did you?"

"Did I what?" Mort was confused.

"Teach him a lesson."

"Oh. No. Never saw him. Eliza said that he came to her place the day before, hollerin' and makin' a fuss, but he was gone before we got there."

"Do you know where he went?"

"How should I know? Probably that filthy rat hole that he calls home."

"So you never saw him the night before the family reunion?"

"Nope, we was all over at Eliza's, playin' cards and drinkin' beer."

"Who all was there playing cards the night?"

"Me, Eliza, her guy Chuck, and my brother Sid."

"The rest of the family wasn't there?"

"Nope. Most of 'em are from downstate. They drove up in the mornin'."

"Were any of them aware of the victim's abusive tendencies?"

"You mean did they know that he used to beat up on her? Nah, only me and Sid knew. The others don't need to be messin' in her personal business."

"Had any of the others met the victim?"

"I don't think so. They had a courthouse weddin' and

none of us went. Me and Sid never liked him," Mort shrugged.

"Did you kill him?" Morgan asked bluntly.

Mort wasn't fazed a bit. "Nope, I didn't, but I'm sure thankful to whoever did."

CHAPTER 8

ROSSIE WAS TORN. She didn't want to press charges against Eliza, but she also didn't want her to think that it was acceptable for her to come into Hawg Heaven ranting and raving, bent on destruction. In the end, she decided to not press charges, but asked Morgan to let Eliza know that if it happened again, she would not only press charges, but would obtain a restraining order.

"It was kind of nice not having Ms. Bouchard around," Garrett mused, as he chopped onions for the breakfast special.

"How come?" José asked, gathering the spices and ingredients that he needed to prepare for the breakfast rush.

"Her boyfriend Chuck stayed there to take care of the boardinghouse, and when we all came down for breakfast, he'd cooked up some really good food, and sat and ate with us. It wasn't uncomfortable like when Ms. Bouchard is there. I always feel like she's watching us, so I usually eat my cereal as fast as I can, then leave."

"Ms. Rossalyn says that she'll be out of jail today and that we're supposed to keep an eye out for her and call the police if she causes trouble."

"I hope she doesn't throw me out," Garrett muttered. "I ain't got nowhere to go."

"If she throws you out, you can crash on my mom's couch until you find a place," José offered.

"Then your mom will throw me out," Garrett smiled sadly.

"Nah, not if you take out the trash, she'll love you forever," José grinned and spun his spatula, turning to the grill.

"Garrett Marshall?" a Chatsworth police officer walked into the kitchen and stood directly in front of the startled young man.

"Yeah?" his eyes went wide.

"I need you to come down to the station with us. We need to question you in connection with the murder of Harlan Howard."

"But I don't know anything about it," Garrett protested, looking to José for support. The lead cook just shrugged helplessly.

"Let's go," the officer directed, his expression brooking no nonsense.

"Yes sir," Garrett hung his head and followed him out the door. "José, please tell Ms. Rossalyn what happened," he mumbled on his way by.

"I will," José said quietly, putting down his spatula and taking his phone out of his pocket.

"You not only helped dig the first pit, you helped construct the cooking area, so you'd know how to disassemble it, and you live on the property. Do you really expect me to believe that you didn't see or hear or do *anything* the night before the body was discovered?" Morgan Tyler asked.

"Officer, that pig weighed a little over 150 pounds. I wouldn't have been able to pull him out of that pit by myself, or lower the body of a man down into it either. Plus, I would've had to dig out the top, which takes a really long time, and someone would've seen me or something. Besides, I don't have any gripe with Mr. Howard. He was awful to Ms. Bouchard, but he never even spoke to me, and from what I heard, she gave as good as she got and sometimes she started it," Garrett explained.

"So you were in bed early, at the boardinghouse, and you didn't hear any noises outside your window at night?"

"No sir, I'm on the second floor and I sleep with the television on. I use earbuds because Ms. Bouchard says I can't have it on after ten o'clock."

"Who else was in the house that night?"

"Well, there's Ms. Bouchard and her brothers and boyfriend, and she has two other guys besides me staying there. Tommy Holmgren just got outta jail a couple weeks ago, he's across the hall from me, and Lester Sauer is in the room next to mine. He's an old guy who can't work anymore, so his social security pays for his room. It's kinda sad."

"Tell me about Tommy," Morgan's eyes flickered.

"He seems to be a nice enough guy," Garrett shrugged. "Tall, huge muscles. I think he spends all of his free time working out. Doesn't say much to anybody, but he's respectful. Even Ms. Bouchard leaves him alone for the most part."

"Has he ever encountered Mr. Howard, to your knowledge?"

"I have no idea."

"Who was at breakfast in the morning, before the reunion?"

"Me, Tommy, Lester, Ms. Bouchard, and Chuck."

Morgan's eyebrows were raised. "Not her brothers?"

"No, sir. I believe they went home the night before."

"What makes you think that?"

"Because they weren't there for breakfast," Garrett blinked at the officer.

"Right," Morgan stared back. "Where are the brothers staying while they're in town?"

"They're at the Iron Post Motel, I think."

"I would think that staying at the boardinghouse would be a much better alternative than the Iron Post. Didn't you say that Eliza has only three boarders right now? That would leave an open room, wouldn't it?"

"Well, yes sir, but sometimes Chuck stays there overnight when he's had a bit too much whiskey."

"He doesn't stay with Eliza?"

"Oh no, sir, she says she don't run that kind of establishment."

"What does she mean by that?"

"I'm sure I don't know, Officer Tyler," Garrett blushed to the roots of his hair.

Morgan sighed. It would shock him to his foundations if Garrett Marshall had anything to do with Harlan Howard's murder, but at least he'd gotten some insight as to the activities within the boardinghouse the night before.

"All right, Garrett, you can go on back to work. I may

need to talk to you again in the next few days, so don't leave town."

"No sir, I won't. Ain't got nowhere to go," he snorted a nervous laugh.

After the young man left, Morgan headed to the office to find out more about Tommy Holmgren.

CHAPTER 9

"WHAT ARE you looking so glum about?" Shelly took Rossalyn's porch steps two at a time and plopped down beside her on the porch swing, her booted feet out in front of her.

"Life. Aren't you working today?" Rossie asked, glad to see her friend, but preoccupied with thoughts of her husband Will.

He'd texted to let her know that he was thinking of her this morning, and it had shaken her to her core. She'd missed him, badly, ever since the two uniformed Marine officers had come to her home on base to break the news of his death, but she couldn't wrap her head around the fact that he hadn't come running back to her the moment that his top-secret assignment finished. She felt betrayed. He had to have known that she and Ryan were suffering, and he still stayed away.

Rossie knew that he'd been badly traumatized, but she was convinced that it would've been easier for him to recover within the warmth of the home and life that they'd built together. He hadn't even given them a chance to help. He'd lived practically like a wild animal for months while she and Ryan made a new life for themselves. Was she just supposed to forgive and forget and start up their lives again? How was that even possible? Her head hurt from the thoughts and guilt tumbling around in her brain. She wanted to be supportive and loving and kind to her husband, but he was a stranger now, and she couldn't figure out what to do.

"Yes, I'm working. But it's my lunch hour, and don't change the subject. You're thinking about Will again, aren't you?"

"Yeah," Rossie propped her arm up on the porch swing and leaned her head into her hand. "I dream about him and it always ends up in nightmares, and I feel guilty."

"You can't help what your subconscious conjures up in dreams. Why on earth would that make you feel guilty?" Shelly asked, puzzled.

Rossie said nothing, but the blush that worked its way up from the base of her neck to the tips of her ears spoke volumes.

"Oh, I see," the firefighter said quietly. "It's not just Will you're dreaming about, is it? Morgan mentioned something about a guy named Tom when we went out to dinner last night. Does he have something to do with this?"

"No," Rossie lied, as her color deepened. "Wait, you went out to dinner with Morgan?"

"Yeah, it wasn't a big deal, we just happened to run into each other on a routine call, and it was right before our dinner break, so we went to the sub sandwich place next to the gas station and had a bite to eat."

"Sounds terribly romantic," Rossie grinned, glad for the subject change.

"Oh my gosh, Morgan Tyler is one smoking hot cop," Shelly practically salivated. "He told me that you shot him down several times when he asked you out," she teased.

"Oh, I did not. I just told him that I wasn't ready to date, and I'm not."

"Uh-huh, sure. Now tell me about this Tom guy," Shelly raised her eyebrows.

"He's a neighbor. A friend. He's helped me and Ryan out more times than I can count. He's a biker who keeps a spotless house and loves dogs."

"And you're into him," Shelly added.

"I am not," Rossie protested, her words sounding hollow, even in her own ears.

If she was being honest with herself, maybe she should just admit that since Will had been back, it had been Tom's advice and company and listening ear that she had missed, not her husband's. Did that make her a terrible person? Maybe, maybe not, but it certainly put her in an awkward position—one that she didn't want to discuss with anyone, including her new bestie.

"Tom is a great guy, and I like him a lot, but I don't need complications in my life right now, you know?"

Shelly watched her friend carefully, seeing the conflicting emotions crossing her features, and decided to change the subject... a bit.

"So where is he?" she asked.

"Who?"

"Tom, the biker."

"Oh, I don't know. I haven't heard from him since just before Will left."

"Hmm... he just took off, huh?"

"Why wouldn't he? For all I know he may be somewhere on business. It's not like he owes me anything."

Shelly heard the hurt behind Rossie's nonchalant reply.

"Business? What does he do for a living?"

"I'm not sure, something on the internet."

"Sounds sketchy. Maybe he came back to town and barbequed Eliza's ex," Shelly chuckled.

"That's disgusting," Rossie made a face.

"Yeah, I crack myself up," Shelly grinned, finally getting a smile out of her friend. "Is there any pizza left from last night?"

"Yep, in the fridge, help yourself."

As Shelly clumped across the front porch in her work boots, stopping to scratch Barney between the ears before heading in the house to microwave some pizza, Rossie was thankful that she'd met her new friend when she did. Sometimes people seemed to come into her life just when she needed them most.

CHAPTER 10

MORGAN TYLER REVIEWED the files on Tommy Holmgren at length.

"Looks like we may just have our guy," he mused, checking out the young man's rap sheet.

Tommy had been bounced around a variety of foster homes since he was born and in and out of legal trouble since he was in junior high school. His mother was a drug addict who left him with friends, neighbors, and anyone else who would feed and clothe him. His paternal grandmother had found him at age two, sitting alone in the dog house, eating dog food, because he'd been left alone for three days. It was anyone's guess where the dog had gone. She'd taken the lice-ridden, soiled toddler to the county crisis center and dropped him off, washing her hands of him. His abusive father had loomed in and out of his life like a grim specter; Tommy's most recent conviction had been for assault, because he'd nearly beaten the old man to a pulp for hitting his mother.

He'd been arrested for just about every petty crime that one could think of, and his pattern indicated that he lied, stole, and cheated more for survival than for any thrill or because he was just a bad kid. He literally used all his resources to survive, and he'd been taught that breaking the law was the way to survive.

Morgan had to analyze the kid's record further, but in the meantime, he was going to bring him in to question him. He hadn't been out of prison for very long; hopefully he'd come clean in order to minimize his time in there this time around.

"Why are there two guys behind you, standing in the corners?" Tommy asked, from across the interrogation table, missing nothing.

"Have you looked in the mirror lately, Tommy?" was Morgan's mild reply.

"I ain't gonna cause no trouble. I just got outta the joint, I ain't lookin' to get back in."

"Good, because I'm hoping that you can help me with some information."

"Information about what?" his eyes narrowed.

"A man was murdered at the boardinghouse a few days ago. I'm sure that you're aware of that."

"Yeah, I wasn't home, but I came here and gave a statement."

"That's right. I'm just trying to clarify a few details surrounding the case, so I'm going to ask you a few more questions."

"Okay," Tommy shrugged.

"The victim's name was Harlan Howard, did you know him?"

Tommy scowled. "Yeah, I knew that good-for-nothin. He reminded me of my old man, the dirtbag."

"Did you ever interact with Mr. Howard when he came to the boardinghouse?"

"Heck, no. If I even saw his truck coming up the drive, I'd take off out the back."

"When was the last time that you had an interaction with Mr. Howard?"

"It's been a long while. I was in jail for six months this last time, and I didn't see him when I came back."

"Where were you on the night of the murder?"

"Joe's Pub. I closed 'em down that night, and blacked out after that."

"Blacked out?" Morgan raised an eyebrow.

"Yeah, that's where you drink too much and can't remember where you were and what you were doing."

"I'm familiar with the concept. What's the next thing that you remember?"

"I woke up the next day in an alley, not smelling too good and with a headache from Hades. When I got back to the house, there were cops all over the place and I couldn't go to my room until I'd given a statement."

"So you have no idea where you were after Joe's closed."

"I'd bet money that I was curled up, sicker than a dog, in that alley."

"Who's your probation officer?"

"Pete Jameson, why?"

"You supposed to be drinking while you're on probation?"

"You know I ain't," Tommy mumbled.

"Tell you what… as long as you continue to cooperate, and don't entertain any plans to leave town, we'll just keep this little conversation between us. But if you step out of line, even this much," Morgan placed his thumb and forefinger a paper's width apart, "we're going to have a problem. You good with that?"

"Yes, sir," Tommy muttered. "Can I go?"

"For now," Morgan stood.

"Hey, Morgan! Long time no see!" Joe Esposito,

owner of Joe's bar, greeted the cop enthusiastically. "I was beginning to think that it would take another bar fight to get you down here," he grinned.

"Hey, Joe, good to see you," Morgan shook his hand and sat on a stool at the bar, where Joe was busy polishing glasses.

"Can I get you something?"

"Just water, I'm on the job."

"Oh? You're seeing me in an official capacity?" his smile dimmed and he stopped toweling down the glass in his hand. "What's up?" he flipped the towel expertly up over his shoulder and set the clean glass on the bar, filling it with ice, water, and a slice of lime.

"You hear about the murder over at the boarding-house?" Morgan asked, taking a long drink.

"You kidding? Everyone in town has heard about that. Eliza Bouchard roasted her old man," Joe shook his head.

"Is that the rumor?"

"That's how I heard it."

"Were you working here the night that it happened?"

Joe cocked his head to the side and thought for a moment. "Well, let's see… I came in for the night shift the day that the body was found, and I took the night shift so that I could sleep in that morning, which means… yep, I worked the night before. I'm almost positive."

"Do you know Tommy Holmgren?"

"Sure, everybody knows Tommy. He in trouble again?"

"That's what I'm trying to find out. He said he was here on the night of the murder, do you remember him being here?"

"I remember seeing him in here, taking shot after shot, all by himself, but I don't remember what night it was. Let me look at my receipts from that night and I'll let you know. He was a cash customer, so his name will be on his tab."

"You gave Tommy a tab when he doesn't have a credit card?" Morgan raised his eyebrows.

"Half the people in this town don't have a credit card, and it's not like I don't know where to find the kid,"

Joe chuckled, pulling out a file box with numbered folders. "Let's see… won't take but a second, I alphabetize the receipts."

"You're very organized," Morgan was impressed.

"This bar is my baby. Gotta do everything just right so she grows," he grinned, pulling out a receipt. "Yep, here it is, he was here that night, sure enough."

"And you served alcohol to a young man on probation?" Morgan raised an eyebrow.

"I figured the kid could probably use a good stiff shot, he's had it pretty rough you know," Joe shrugged.

"That's what I've heard. Do you remember how long he stayed?"

"He got good and drunk, but I didn't worry because I know that he doesn't have a car, and he left around closing time."

"Do you know where he went after that?"

"Home I would guess, but I couldn't swear to it."

"Do you have security cameras?"

"Security cameras? In Chatsworth?" Joe laughed.

"Yeah, I figured. Just thought I'd ask. Were you the only one working that night?"

"Anna Marie was here for the happy hour crowd, but she left around nine. I closed up by myself."

"Gotcha." Morgan drained his ice water and thanked Joe, then headed for the door.

He had no way of checking out Tommy's story. Joe had verified his claims of getting drunk, but unless he found a witness who could testify to seeing him passed out in the alley, his story was looking rather thin. Had the young man snapped, his scars from the past overriding his good sense?

Morgan didn't know, but he knew one thing… Tommy was a body builder, and body builders typically metabolized alcohol pretty quickly, which meant he theoretically could've been staggering drunk when he left the bar, and sober enough to murder a man by the time he walked home.

CHAPTER 11

Tommy Holmgren was mad at the world. It seemed as though everything and everyone was out to get him, so he did what he'd seen modeled in front of him his whole life and got drunk. Staggering, stinking, sloppy drunk. He'd been ready for a fight, and had been politely but firmly asked to leave Joe's Bar around ten o'clock. It had taken a free burger and fries (to go), to get him out the door without a ruckus, but he eventually went, pawing the food into his mouth like an animal as he stumbled down the street.

He instinctively headed back to the boardinghouse, with the goal of making it to his bed before he passed out, but he was stopped on the front porch by Eliza, who was, as usual, smoking a cigarette.

"Just where do you think you're going, mister?" she stood up and put a hand out so that he couldn't make it up the porch steps. He might not have been able to anyway, but Eliza wasn't taking any chances.

"What, you gonna hassle me too?" he slurred, swaying a bit and holding onto the porch railing.

"You know I got rules. Ain't no drunkenness in this house, ain't no vomiting on my wood floors. You just find yourself another place to sleep tonight, Tommy Holmgren," Eliza stood, hands on hips, blocking the steps, cigarette hanging from her lips.

"Yeah, you're just like all the rest. You don't care. Put me out in the street and let me die," Tommy mumbled, his eyes on his shoes.

"Oh, cry me a river, tough guy. You made your choices in life, you live with 'em, and that includes choosing to throw some cheap whiskey down your gullet until you can hardly see. You're gonna be payin' for that choice for a while. Now go on, go find somewhere to sleep it off. It's a summer night, you ain't gonna die of exposure. Skeeters ain't even gonna bite you, you're so full of whiskey," Eliza shook her head.

"My momma never hugged me," Tommy muttered, not looking up.

"What? That's bull, everybody's mama hugs 'em, even the bad ones," her voice was a bit softer, and she took a long drag from her cigarette, blowing the smoke out audibly, its end glowing in the summer night.

"No. She never did. She didn't like me, half the time she was so out of it that she didn't even know me," he shook his head and staggered back a bit as a result. "My daddy just beat up on both of us. I don't know why she kept coming back for more, but she did, and she never paid me no attention."

Eliza tossed her half-finished cigarette onto the ground and smashed it with her flip-flop. "Don't make no sense, does it?" she murmured dully. "We don't know why we go back either. Just always hopin' it'll get better, I s'pose, or maybe not havin' anywhere else to go. It's awful lonely being in a relationship by yourself and draggin' a hateful man along," she made a face, her tone bitter.

"Why wouldn't she just be nice to me?" Tommy glanced up, his eyes haunted by past pain.

"She couldn't," Eliza answered, a faraway look in her eyes. "She had nothin' left. He killed it all. Any spark of her that was left, he put it out, leaving her just... empty."

"Miss Eliza?"

When she broke out of her reverie, she noticed that Tommy was close enough for her to smell the whiskey on his breath. She also noticed that his wide, dark eyes were fringed with lashes that were long and thick. She noticed the sculpted muscle of his body beneath his t-shirt, and she noticed that he was bending his head down to kiss her. She let him.

Rossalyn Channing slept well, with Barney snoring on the floor beside her bed, despite still being bothered by the hog roast murder. That the police had even questioned Garrett more thoroughly than others spiked her protective instincts. She knew that he was a good kid and hated that he'd had to go through an interrogation, although he'd said that it hadn't been that bad.

Feeling refreshed for the first time in days, Rossie

took Barney for a short walk, and was surprised when her phone buzzed in her pocket. Who on earth would be calling her at this hour? She didn't want to look at the phone, thinking that it might be Will, and she didn't know what to say to him just yet, but, since Ryan was away and in a different time zone, she did. Her heart sank when she saw José's number on the screen—he would never call her in the morning unless something was wrong at Hawg Heaven.

"José, everything okay?" she answered, holding Barney's leash in one hand and her phone in the other.

"No, Miss Rossalyn. Hawg Heaven was robbed," the cook was breathless. "I just got here and the door was open. They emptied the cash drawer that was locked in your desk and took the change from the charity jar," he explained. "I called the police and then I called you."

"Oh my gosh, José! Are you okay? Were they still there when you arrived?" Rossie's adrenaline shot through the roof.

"No, they were gone, I'm still shaking, but I'm fine. Should I start prepping for breakfast? I don't know what to do," he admitted.

"No, sweetie, don't even worry about it. Just sit tight until the police get there and I'll be right over."

The police came, took a report and dusted for fingerprints, requesting that Rossie keep Hawg Heaven closed for the day so that they could do a full investigation.

"Any idea who might do such a thing?" the officer who had been the first to arrive asked.

Rossie sighed. "The only one that I can think of is a customer who thinks that I owe her a refund."

"Eliza Bouchard?" the officer asked.

Rossie gave him a surprised look. "How…?" she began.

"Everybody knows how Eliza can be. She's got a wicked temper, and her feathers are ruffled right now. I don't know that she'd ever break the law, but we'll check it out. With you being this close to the highways, it was more likely just somebody drifting through. Might want to think about a security system eventually."

"I thought people didn't need security systems in small towns," Rossie sighed.

"People are people no matter where you go, Ms. Channing. We're gonna talk to José for a little bit, see if he saw any details that might be helpful, then you folks can head on home. It'll take us some time to go through the scene."

"Thank you," Rossie replied, feeling numb.

Morgan Tyler wasn't looking forward to yet another trip out to Eliza's boardinghouse, but after the burglary at Hawg Heaven had been reported, he knew that she needed to be questioned very carefully, so he'd volunteered to do it, much to the relief of the responding officer. Talking to Eliza Bouchard was like trying to cuddle a cactus: no matter how careful you were, there was always the risk of getting stuck.

He pulled his patrol car into the drive and got out in a hurry when he saw a fight move out of the doorway and into the side yard. Two very large men were going at it in a manner that would land one or the other in the hospital, or worse.

"Hey!" Morgan shouted, running toward the men. "Police, freeze!" he hollered again, trying to step into the fray as punches were thrown and bodies were flung violently against one another. "Don't make me bust out the mace, boys," he warned.

If either man heard him, neither showed it, so Morgan stepped back and had just uncapped his pepper spray, when he recognized who the fighters were, much to his astonishment.

"Chuck Lantman!" Morgan bellowed, really not wanting to use the spray unless he absolutely had to.

He'd intentionally called out the name of the most rational man in the fight, in hopes of defusing it. Chuck glanced back at him, wiping a trickle of blood from the corner of his eye while holding off an extremely agitated Tommy Holmgren with the other.

"This don't involve you, Tyler," Chuck grunted, landing a punch just under Tommy's ribs and spurring on another barrage of blows from the younger man.

"It does now. You're breaking the law," Morgan shouted to be heard among the blows. "You either quit, or I'm gonna spray you down hard and take you both in. What's it gonna be, Chuck?"

Eliza's boyfriend gritted his teeth, executed a spin

move and in a heartbeat had Tommy's wrists pinned up between his shoulder blades, shoving him down to the ground.

"Hold him right there," Morgan ordered, pulling a zip tie out of a cargo pocket and securing Tommy's hands with it.

"That's right, loser," Chuck growled, sneering at the prone young man.

"Now get down on your knees with your hands above your head," the officer told an outraged Chuck.

"Are you kidding me? I just contained him for you."

"I've still got the spray in my hand, Chuck, and I still don't want to use it, but I will," Morgan said quietly.

Seeing his resolve, Chuck sank to his knees, hands above his head, both he and Tommy still trying to catch their breath. Once Morgan had zip-tied his wrists behind his back, he helped each of the sweating, filthy, and bloodied men to a sitting position.

"Who the heck called the cops?" Eliza demanded, impatiently tying the sash of her worn terrycloth robe together. "You were here before they even took it outside," her eyes narrowed at Morgan.

"I'm here on a different matter," the officer dismissed her and turned his attention to the fighters. "You boys want to tell me what the heck is going on here?"

"I've got breakfast to attend to," Eliza muttered and beat a hasty retreat.

"Ain't none of your business, Morgan," Chuck growled, his eyes on the ground.

"Disturbing the peace at this hour of the morning made it my business. You want to explain yourselves here or do I need to take you in?"

"It's personal," Tommy mumbled, and Chuck shot him a venomous look.

"Lover's tiff?" Morgan's tone dripped sarcasm.

"Something like that," Chuck replied, his jaw clenched.

The officer looked from one to the other and back again. Tommy looked ashamed and miserable, and Chuck was clearly barely able to suppress his rage.

"You two gonna work this out amongst yourselves, without raising a ruckus?" Morgan demanded, realizing that something had gone down here that he really didn't want to be privy to.

"Yeah," Tommy said, not raising his head.

"Chuck, if I let you go, are you going to get out of here without any trouble and not come back until you've cooled off?" the officer stared him down.

"Might never come back," Chuck ground out, his breath whistling through his nose.

"That's entirely up to you. I'm gonna walk you to your truck, then take off the zip tie and you're going to get in and drive away, are we agreed?"

"Yeah," he snapped, a vein on his forehead pulsing.

"If you make a move other than that, I'm gonna pepper spray you, understood?"

"Just get me outta here."

Morgan turned to Tommy. "You stay put and keep your mouth shut until he's driving away, got it?"

"Yeah," Tommy's gaze hadn't strayed from the spot at his feet during the entire interaction.

"You sick or something?" Morgan asked.

Before Tommy could answer, Chuck did. "Yeah, he's something all right."

"Let's go," Morgan helped Chuck to his feet, walked him to the truck and removed the zip ties, standing between Chuck and Tommy until Chuck climbed up into the cab of his truck, started it, and drove away.

"I'm gonna be sick," Tommy groaned.

"Well, wait until I get your hands free, then go do what you need to do," Morgan trotted over and quickly released him.

He went to the front door and knocked, hearing the sounds of a very uncomfortable Tommy spewing into the bushes, while Eliza let him in.

"Where were you last night after eight o'clock, Eliza?"

"Ain't none of your business where I was, Morgan Tyler," she slurped at the mug of coffee in her hand.

"There's been some trouble in town, Eliza, and whether you like it or not, if you don't have an alibi, I might be taking you to jail again," he threatened.

"Trouble? What kind of trouble?"

"Doesn't matter. Where were you last night after eight?" Morgan repeated, trying not to lose patience.

"Fine, I was here, are you happy now?"

"Is there anyone who can corroborate that?"

Eliza shot him a glare. "You calling me a liar?"

"Not at all, I just need to know whether anyone saw you and can verify that you were here."

"Lester was home," her eyes avoided his.

"Did he actually come out of his room after eight o'clock and see you here?"

Eliza's lips tightened. "No, but I'm sure he heard me cleaning the kitchen and such."

"That doesn't prove anything. It could've been anyone cleaning the kitchen," Morgan pointed out.

Eliza stared at him for a moment, then let out a sigh, defeated. "Tommy," she said, not looking at the cop.

"What about Tommy?"

"He can vouch for me being here."

"Did he see you here?"

"Yeah, he was with me," she colored, still avoiding Morgan's eyes.

"I… see," the officer cleared his throat. "Was he here all evening?"

"No. He got here just after ten, and… knew that I was here… the rest of the night. Not that it's any of your business, and don't you go spreading that all over town either, Morgan Tyler," she muttered.

"Chuck came over this morning and found Tommy… with you," he guessed.

"That's the long and short of it, yeah."

"I'm gonna have a little talk with Tommy before I leave."

"Good luck with that," Eliza snorted. "Boy can't hold his liquor, he's been green as my ivy plant all morning."

"I'll be in touch."

"Can't wait," Eliza drawled, turning away and heading to the kitchen for more coffee.

CHAPTER 12

To say that Tom Hundman was massive would be a bit of an understatement. He was unforgettably tall, with rippling muscles filling out his sizeable frame. He wore his dark hair long, and his beard was thick, giving him the appearance of a motorcycle-riding pirate. His eyes were the kind of blue that made you shiver a bit, whether you were the subject of either his ire or his interest, and the Marine vet had seen too much and done too much to be entirely comfortable in polite company. To his few friends, he was loyal to the death; his enemies, if they were smart, stayed far away; and most folks he just avoided whenever possible.

The biker pounded on Mort Bouchard's door at the

Iron Post Motel with a point and purpose and the older man paled significantly when he craned his neck to gaze up at Tom.

"Where's the money, Mort?" Tom demanded quietly, grabbing him by the throat and pushing him backwards into the shabby room, where Sid sat, watching TV and eating a microwaved corndog.

"I don't know what you're talking about," he gasped, his face reddening as Tom slowly began to squeeze.

"One more time, Mort… where's the money?" Tom asked, his nose mere inches from the now-purpling face.

"… Don't… know," Mort grunted, as stars swam in front of his eyes.

"Hey!" Sid rose from his recliner, chewing. Tom shot him a look and he sat back down, watching.

Tom squeezed harder and Mort began to flail.

"Hey, stop it Hundman! I'll tell you where the money is, just don't kill my brother," Sid pleaded.

Tom turned to look at him and opened his hand,

causing Mort to drop to the floor, clutching his neck and drawing in ragged and painful breaths.

"Start talking, little man, or you're next," the biker stepped over Mort, toward Sid.

"He gave it to her. He gave it to Eliza," Sid's eyes shifted toward Mort, who was trying to give him a signal of some kind.

Tom crossed his arms over his broad chest and raised an eyebrow. "I wasn't born yesterday, idiot. You tell me where it is right now, or I'm gonna leave you both in so many pieces that they won't be able to tell who is who."

"Toilet," Mort croaked, then winced.

"Toilet?" Tom repeated, looking at Sid, who looked as though the wind had just left his sails.

"Yeah," he sighed. "Come on, back here," he led the biker toward the bathroom, which smelled of mildew and looked as though it hadn't had a thorough cleaning since the place opened in the seventies.

Mort crawled over and sat up against the side of one of the beds, catching his breath and rubbing his throat, while Sid went into the filthy bathroom and lifted the lid from the tank behind the toilet. Inside, stashed in a plastic bag from the local grocery store, was roughly two hundred and fifty dollars in cash, the sum total of Rossie's cash drawer. Sid handed it over to Tom, who stared at him in a manner that made him wonder if he'd ever see the light of day again.

"She shelled out the money for the family reunion. We just wanted to help her out, that's all. She said that fancy pants lady could afford it better than she could," Mort rasped, his eyes glassy and red.

"I'm only gonna say this once, so you better listen up," Tom said in a deadly quiet voice. "You two are gonna get in that piece of junk rustbucket out there and you're gonna drive to the police station. I'll be right behind you, and if you do anything but drive directly there, I will find you." He let that sink in for a moment before continuing. "If I ever, and I mean ever, hear that you've said anything or done anything bad to or about Rossalyn Channing, you'll regret it for the rest of your miserable lives. Got it?"

Mort nodded, his throat too sore to speak, and Sid gulped and cleared his throat before saying yes.

"Where's Tyler?" Tom Hundman demanded when he got to the police station, pushing Mort and Sid in ahead of him.

The two brothers had a hangdog look about them that reminded the aging desk clerk of two boys who'd gotten caught with their hands in the cookie jar.

"He's out at Eliza's boardinghouse, but I don't expect he'll be there too long. Just taking a statement. You wanna wait?"

"More than anything." Tom rolled his eyes and shoved the brothers toward the small waiting area, where they sat obediently in ancient molded plastic chairs the color of green olives.

"Don't you sass me, Mister. I changed your britches when your mama was working nights at the donut shop to put food in your mouth," the clerk reminded him. Ida Mae Fernley was a fixture in Chatsworth, having spent seemingly her entire life behind the counter at the police station.

The Bouchard brothers snickered a bit at that, but Tom silenced them with a look. "Let him know I have a couple of no-good thieves who might just be murderers sitting in his lobby."

Ida Mae blinked at him. "Them two?" her eyebrows shot toward her hairline.

"Yeah, them."

The clerk pursed her lips for a moment, then shook her head. "All right, I'll just send him a text."

Tom leaned against the tall counter as she painstakingly picked out the letters of her text with one forefinger, squinting at her cellphone like it was an alien device.

"There," she smiled triumphantly when she finally hit send. "Now we'll just wait for him to respond. Go sit down and quit cluttering up my counter," she shooed the massive biker away.

Mort and Sid eyed him warily, each hoping that he didn't choose to sit by them, in case something happened to set off his notorious temper.

The office phone rang and Ida Mae picked up.

"Chatsworth PD. Oh, hey Morgan, did you get my text? They aren't? You will? Are you sure? That just doesn't sound right. Okay, will do. Be safe."

She hung up the phone and headed toward the back, returning shortly with a uniformed officer.

"Bart here is gonna detain these two gentlemen while you provide me with a statement," she told Tom.

As the cop took the Bouchard brothers back to a holding cell, Tom gave Ida Mae a long look. "Where is Morgan?" he asked.

"On his way to arrest a murderer from what he said. It might be a while. Now you just write down all about what them Bouchard boys have been up to," she handed him a clipboard with a form on it, and a pen with the cap chewed. "Soon as Bart comes back, he'll go through it with you."

"Ain't gonna tell me where Morgan went, are you?" Tom accepted the clipboard.

"Nope," she shook her head firmly.

"Why?"

"It's official police business, and it don't involve you. Now just go write down your statement."

CHAPTER 13

MORGAN TYLER HAD PULLED his patrol car into the private lane, but had parked it behind a stand of trees, where it wouldn't be visible from the road or the house. Heat baked into the black polyester blend of his uniform, and burs clung to his socks, irritating his ankles. As he made his way carefully toward the house, droplets of sweat trickled down his neck and spine.

Crouching behind a pair of out-of-control yews, which looked as though they hadn't been pruned since they were planted, Morgan surveyed the yard and house, from the back corner of the lot. He hadn't approached from the front, because if it came down to a confrontation, he wanted to have the element of surprise on his side. The windows were closed, and a rickety air-conditioner was running full-blast, which was good, because it would mask sound. The detached garage stood between Morgan and the house, a perfect scenario, because the garage was the first thing he wanted to search. While he couldn't enter a locked and secured area without a warrant, if the garage door just happened to be open, he could go inside and take a look around. Anything that was in obvious sight of a casual passerby was fair game, and he wanted to substantiate his hunch before approaching the suspect.

With a fleeting thought that he should have called for backup, just in case, Morgan darted out from behind the yews to the back of the garage, then slid around the far corner of it, keeping low and close to the exterior wall. Luck was on his side. He'd been betting that there was a door on the right-hand side, near the back, because he saw a spigot there, with a sprinkler hooked up to it. His guess was right on the money, and fate smiled upon him even further, the door was open a crack. He put his ear to it, hoping that his luck would hold and that the structure would be unoccupied.

After listening for what seemed like hours, but was really only a couple of minutes, Morgan pushed on the door to ease it open and winced when it creaked like it had been there for a hundred years. Motionless, he listened again, and snuck peeks around the corner to see if anyone in the house had heard the sound. When all was clear, he swung it open far enough for him to slip inside. With one last glance toward the house, he shimmied into the narrow opening, touching as little as possible.

Thankful for the daylight pouring into the garage, he found what he'd come to see, and went straight toward the old blue pickup truck. There was a gun rack, and on it, the same caliber of rifle that had been used to put a bullet in Harlan Howard before he was thrown into the roasting pit. There were greasy hand-prints along the sides of the bed, and tiny chunks of what sure looked like pork caught on bolt heads inside the bed. Moving around to the tailgate, Morgan saw strands that looked like they'd come from a burlap sack, and glancing over in the corner of the garage, he saw a shovel with dirt and ashes on the business end of it, as well as smeared along the handle.

In the other half of the garage, next to the truck, was a

fully loaded weight bench and personal gym, where the killer had apparently worked out in order to prepare for the heinous act which had been committed. Morgan now knew that he'd come to the right place, and steeled himself for the meeting that was about to follow. He rose from his crouch in front of the shovel, and when he stood, he heard the back door to the house slam. Ducking back down, he went to the window and saw the suspect striding quickly toward the garage.

Eliza Bouchard was madder than a wet hen, and Ida Mae wasn't budging an inch.

Twitching for a cigarette, the little woman ranted and railed at the placid-faced woman behind the desk.

"As if it ain't bad enough that y'all believed that stupid biker when he said he saw my brothers robbing little Ms. Sugarbritches, then you gotta pile it on by accusing Chuck of murder and locking him up like a common criminal? You people better learn how to do your jobs. I swear to you, Ida Mae, you better let me back there to see Chuck right now, or I'm gonna cause a ruckus. That man wouldn't hurt a fly," Eliza insisted, leaning over the counter toward the immovable clerk.

"His rap sheet would indicate otherwise, and don't you even think about threatening me or telling me how to do my job, you little midge. I'll have somebody come out here and throw you in a cage, too."

"He's innocent," Eliza hollered.

"He confessed, dimwit, and you ain't got nothing to say about it. Morgan got enough evidence to put him under the jail. The bed of that boy's pickup truck had pork and grease all over it, his shovel had ashes from the pit on it, your ex's blood was on the sole of his work boots, and the slug that killed the victim matches his gun. Sorry, honey, you're gonna just have to find another squeeze to keep you warm at night." Ida Mae had clearly had enough. "Now get on outta here before I have to call one of the boys to come handcuff you," she ordered.

Eliza's mouth dropped open and she gaped wordlessly at the grandmotherly looking woman who had just given her the worst news that she'd heard in quite some time.

"He really did it?" she whispered.

Ida Mae nodded, shocked to see Eliza's eyes welling with tears. She hadn't thought the feisty little woman had any tender feelings in her.

"Self-defense… it had to be self-defense, right?" she grasped at straws.

"Sorry, hon, your ex was shot in the back of the head. There ain't no judge in the world who's gonna believe that was self-defense. It was murder, plain and simple. Chuck said he couldn't stand to see Harlan hurting you no more," Ida Mae's voice was softer.

"Wouldn't you just know it," Eliza shook her head bitterly, absently rubbing her upper arms. "Finally find a decent man who treats me good and he screws it up."

"He had a violent past, Eliza. Seems like it might've only been a matter of time before something happened to you."

"Well I sure as heck know how to pick 'em, don't I? I'm done with men. I'm gonna run my business and live my life, and heaven help the man who tries to get friendly with me. I'm done with all of 'em."

A tear escaped her eye and she dashed it away bitterly.

CHAPTER 14

Rossie held in her hands an entire box of José's renowned double-chocolate, bacon caramel brownies. The gooey, luscious treats were served on Fridays, and because of them, there was a line that formed in front of the door before they even opened. On holidays, locals ordered dozens of them and were willing to pay a premium price for the decadent creations.

Taking a deep breath, she knocked softly on her neighbor's back door, still not knowing fully what she was doing or expecting. Within seconds, she heard the clomp of heavy motorcycle boots as Tom Hundman made his way to the door.

"Yeah?" he asked, looking impatient.

Rossalyn could have sworn that she saw a look cross his features before his aloof mask slipped into place. Had it been pain? What could've happened to him when he disappeared after Will came to town? She realized how little she knew about the enigmatic biker, despite the fact that they'd become more at ease with each other recently.

"Uh, hi," Rossie was baffled by his manner, particularly after they'd been getting to know each other a bit better in the weeks before Will came back. "I... umm... wanted to say thank you for catching the guys who broke into Hawg Heaven, so I brought you some of José's famous double-chocolate, bacon caramel brownies. I had to watch out for bandits on the way over, these things are so popular," she laughed nervously, wondering what was wrong with her... and him.

"Not necessary," his voice was toneless and he moved to shut the door.

On impulse, Rossalyn stuck her foot in the way, and he looked up, surprised. "Is everything okay?" she asked. "I mean, you kinda disappeared and then you saved the day... again... and I just... will you come over and have a brownie with me at least? Ryan is with his grandparents and it's just so quiet with me and Barney," she blushed, not having anticipated issuing an impromptu invitation.

Tom looked pointedly down at her foot, which was still preventing him from closing the door. "Nah, I can't." His face was like stone, which pierced her newly-fragile psyche.

Her reaction to pain, as seemed typical these days, was white-hot anger, but she fought to remain calm.

"Why?" she demanded. "We're neighbors, for crying out loud. You did something nice for me, and I'd like to show you a little appreciation. Is it too much to ask for you to come over and just eat a darn brownie? I'm sorry if I'm such bad company that you can't stand to be in my presence."

Her chin began to tremble a bit and she clenched her teeth to still it. She wouldn't give him the satisfaction of seeing her cry at his rejection. He closed his eyes briefly, and when he opened them again, she couldn't fathom his expression, but for some reason, it made her heart hurt even worse.

"Rossalyn, you're a married woman. It wouldn't be right for you to be keeping company with another man while you're trying to figure out what to do about your marriage. I left because I thought that it would be better for both of us if you did some thinking without me around," he said quietly.

"What if my thinking included thoughts of you?" she whispered, feeling vulnerable to the extreme.

The pained look flashed again, then was gone. "I shouldn't have come back. You gotta finish one book before you start reading another, whether there's a happily ever after or not. You've put a bookmark in it and set it on the nightstand, and that doesn't do anybody any good. Talk to him, see what you want, make a decision. Then maybe I'll come over for a brownie."

His words, while painful, were wise and true, and as Rossie listened, a tear trailed slowly down her cheek. She was so absorbed in him that she neither noticed it, nor cared. She wordlessly offered him the box of brownies, and he took them, his eyes locked with hers. Rossie pulled her foot back and he quietly shut the door while she stood on his porch, staring at the floorboards for a few minutes before turning to go.

A soft summer rain began to fall as she trudged

toward home, her feet taking her where she needed to go, while her thoughts were a million miles away. The light precipitation had turned into a steadily falling rain by the time she reached her back porch, and she sank down on the steps, rivulets of rain mixing with the flow of her tears.

CHAPTER 15

"Do what you need to do, Rossie," Margo counseled, her heart aching for her daughter. "We'll extend our California trip for as long as you need us to. Ryan is having a great time out here."

"Thanks, Mom," Rossalyn's breath hitched.

She hadn't slept all night. She'd paced in her room until she thought she'd go crazy, then she'd sat at the breakfast bar in the kitchen drinking herbal tea to try to get to sleep, but once she'd finished two cups, she found herself wandering aimlessly around the living room, lost in thought. Tom was right. She'd been burying her head in the sand and pushing thoughts of her husband away so that she didn't have to deal with them, but she couldn't really move forward in her life until she'd given herself, and Will, some sort of resolution. She didn't know yet what that resolution would be, but she knew that she had to go see him, talk to him, and put aside her fears long enough for them to decide how they wanted to move forward with their lives.

Pulling Chas Beckett's card out of her purse, glad that she had kept it when the private investigator, his associate Spencer, and her husband had all left Chatsworth together, she checked the name of the town that she couldn't remember. Calgon, Florida. Dreading the thought of a trip to Florida in late summer, she nevertheless did an internet search and found a beautiful bed and breakfast inn on the beach. She took a deep breath, picked up the phone and made a reservation with a friendly woman named Carla. There, it was done. She'd committed to go to Florida. She made an airline reservation next, solidifying her resolve, then hung up the phone and started packing without much thought, tearfully tossing clothing into her suitcase. She'd talked to Shelly after speaking with her mother, and the firefighter would be house- and Barney-sitting while she was gone. José, Garrett, and Ashley would run Hawg Heaven, knowing that Rossie was available by phone if they needed her. There were no more excuses; it was time to be an adult and face her future.

Knowing that she was only postponing the inevitable, Rossalyn decided to take a day for herself after checking into the Beach House B&B in Calgon. She planned to spend some time on the beach, thinking about what she might want to say, and how to say it. The inn had provided her with a lounger, a cooler of drinks and snacks, towels, and an umbrella. Rossie had spent her morning walking along the beach, the warm salt water lapping at her ankles while the Florida sun kissed her skin.

"Hot in Florida feels way better than hot in Illinois," she murmured, tilting her sun hat down over her eyes and slipping into sleep in the lounger.

She had no idea how long she slept, but she woke up feeling better. Hungry and thirsty, but better. She had a long drink of sparkling water with a delicate slice of lime, then noticed that, a short walk away, just off of the beach, was a cute little cupcake shop. She wanted to stretch her legs again, and anticipated the taste of a fluffy little sugar bomb with glee. Real food didn't appeal to her right now, but the idea of a cupcake made her mouth water and her stomach growl. Leaving behind the cooler of fruit, cheese, and crackers, she pulled on her beach cover-up and headed for the shop.

"Well, good mornin'!" a blonde woman with a sweet smile and a charming southern accent greeted her.

"Hi," Rossie tried to return the smile, almost succeeding. "I hope it's okay to come in dressed like this. I was on the beach and had a craving."

"Oh, of course, honey. Happens all the time. Want some coffee while you decide on which cupcakes you'd like?"

"Oh, I'd love that, thank you."

"So, are you staying at the inn?" the woman asked, while pouring a steaming hot cup of coffee.

"Yes, I am," Rossie seated herself at a bistro table that was painted pistachio green, and gazed into a glass case filled with luscious-looking cupcakes.

"You'll love Carla, she's the best. Where are you from?"

"Illinois."

"How nice! I was just in Illinois a few months back. Town called Champaign. Which part of Illinois are you from?"

"Further north. A little town that no one has ever heard of, Chatsworth."

The blonde woman froze, then frowning, lifted up a glass cake tray that had several cupcakes on it. Extracting two, and lost in thought, she put them on a tray and set them down in front of Rossie.

"These are the cupcakes of the day. On the house. Did you say Chatsworth?" she asked, her face serious.

"Yes, do you know it?" Rossie was surprised, and a bit alarmed at the woman's sudden behavioral change.

"Sort of. This is a long shot, but do you happen to know a man named Will Channing?" she asked softly.

The color drained from Rossie's face. "He's my husband," she whispered. "But how…?"

"You must be the beautiful Rossalyn," the woman's face was full of compassion. "I'm Missy Beckett, and my husband Chas met you a few weeks ago."

"Small world," Rossie murmured, stunned.

She gripped her cup of coffee tightly in both hands and took a small sip, her stomach clenching in reaction to hearing her husband's name.

"Will seems like a good man. Troubled, but good."

"How do you know him?"

"He's working with my husband and his associate, Spencer Bengal. Spencer and Will knew each other from... their previous line of work. Those two went through some tough things together."

Rossie nodded.

"I can't even imagine what it must be like for you to suddenly have him reappear, after grieving for him for so long." Missy poured herself a cup of coffee and sat down across from Rossalyn. "How are you handling that?"

Rossie barked a nervous laugh. "Not very well, I'm afraid."

Her voice broke on the last word and she stared down into her cup.

"You poor thing," Missy sighed. "Have you talked to anyone about this?"

"My mom, my friend Shelly," Rossie shrugged, not trusting herself to look into Missy's concerned eyes, fearing that she'd break down.

"I'm talking about a professional, darlin'," Missy said gently, pushing the plate of cupcakes closer to Rossie. "Take a bite, you need some sugar in you," she encouraged. Rossalyn obliged and nibbled at one of the picture-perfect cakes, her eyes widening a bit at the amazing explosion of flavor.

"You mean, like, a psychologist or something" she asked, chewing slowly, and forcing herself to swallow. Even delicious food seemed to turn to sawdust in her mouth these days.

"Sometimes a good therapist can help you see things objectively when you're too close."

"I'd never even considered that," Rossie raised her eyebrows.

"Seems that you're a little bit like me," Missy smiled. "Always trying to handle everything on your own. It took me a long time to trust anyone enough to share. My parents were killed in a car accident when I was seventeen. I took over their cupcake shop and still finished my education. I pushed folks away who only wanted to help, but I was in over my head and didn't realize it. I never would have made it without some help."

"That's kind of what it was like after I thought that Will had died," Rossie nodded and her eyes filled with tears. "My parents were there for me, but I was determined to make a life for myself and my son Ryan on my own. Then I was helped over and over when I opened my café," she murmured, thinking of Tom and José and Garrett, even Morgan.

"It really gives you a new perspective on things when you finally let your guard down and let folks pitch in, doesn't it?" Missy asked, watching her new friend carefully.

"Letting my guard down," Rossie repeated, mechanically taking a bite of her cupcake. "I haven't been doing that. I've been on guard with my own husband," she realized, sitting up straighter. "Why would I do that?"

"My guess is because you were hurt so profoundly

when you thought you lost him, that you don't want to go through that again. Love is full of risks, Rossalyn, but they're so worth it," Missy assured her.

Rossie stared at her. "How is it that I'm having this conversation with a total stranger? You must be the easiest person in the world to talk to," she grinned wanly.

Missy chuckled. "Oh honey, I'm a judgment-free zone because I've been through the wringer and made more silly mistakes than I can count. I have to ask you though, are you sitting here in my cupcake shop avoiding your husband?"

"Of course I am," Rossie admitted. "I just don't know what to say to him."

"Then maybe you shouldn't say anything. Maybe you should listen."

Rossie blinked at her and nodded. "I can do that."

CHAPTER 16

WILL Channing was more nervous than he had been when they'd raided government offices in the Middle East. He'd gotten a haircut, so the long locks that he'd used to avoid humanity were gone, and he was clean shaven. With the exception of the scars of war still prominent on his face, he looked much more like Will Channing than Darryl Janssen, his government-assigned name for covert work.

Spencer had tried to get him to wear a suit for the meeting with his wife, but he'd refused. That wasn't how Rossie would have remembered him. He wore a casual button-down shirt, and plaid shorts, his style from before. From before his life had been turned upside down by a special assignment that no amount of reasoning had been able to get him out of, despite his having a wife and kid. He wanted to look as much like the Will Channing that she remembered as possible. If things went well, he wanted to take her to dinner afterwards, but at this stage of the game, he had his doubts about whether he'd be able to eat a bite. He wanted nothing more than to pull her close and kiss her like he used to, but just the thought scared him. He hadn't been that vulnerable with another human being for quite some time, and didn't know if he'd be able to go back to that kind of openness with any real success.

Will sat on the park bench, bouncing his knees up and down nervously, holding a bouquet of pink roses so tightly that he had compressed the stems into a single thick unit. Then he saw her. She looked incredibly beautiful as she walked up the sidewalk toward him, the summer breeze catching the gauzy folds of her skirt and swirling it around her. How he'd missed those eyes... her hair... he only wished that she would smile her special smile, but uncertainty shrouded her features instead. He stood and handed her the flowers, not knowing what to do. His normal greeting would have been a hug and kiss, but he had no idea how that would be received, so he put his hands in his pockets instead.

"Hi," she said, biting her lip the way she used to when she was nervous or afraid.

"Hi, Rossie," his words were soft, caressing her the way his hands could not.

"It's good to see you," she surprised him by saying.

"You too," he was at a loss as to how to proceed. "Wanna take a walk?"

She nodded. "I'd like that."

The awkward formality of their interaction was killing him inside. She was his wife and he yearned for her. The fact that she'd come down to Florida to see him was encouraging, but he still wondered whether she'd be better off without him. They walked along in silence for a while, with Rossalyn occasionally lifting the roses and breathing in their fragrance.

"I don't know what to say, Will," she said finally, glancing up at him as they walked.

His heart sunk, wondering if this was a prelude to her final goodbye.

"That makes two of us."

"Can you tell me what you're thinking?" she asked, just like she used to do. It nearly brought tears to his eyes as memories of their talks flooded through him.

"So many things," he replied. "I want you to know what I'm dealing with right now, and it might be hard to hear, but before you decide what you want to do, you deserve to know," he began, courageously taking her hand and leading her to a park bench, where they both sat, looking out over a small duck pond.

"Okay," she nodded. "Go ahead, you can tell me anything."

Will gazed out over the water, a muscle in the side of his face twitching. "Right now my mind is all over the place. I'm thinking about you, and how you've always been the most beautiful woman I've ever known, inside and out. I'm also looking at that clump of bushes over there," he inclined his head, "because they'd be a perfect place for the enemy to hide. That bump in the grass could easily be an IED," he pointed, referring to the bombs that he'd come in contact with while in war zones. "I've identified the three best vantage points for sniper fire, and I've scanned the area for the best places to take cover," he shook his head bitterly.

"It's with me, Rossie. Everywhere I go, I can't shake the thoughts, the instincts. My heart is with you and how I feel and how much I love and miss you, and my head keeps looking for ways to keep you safe and defeat an enemy that isn't even there," the veteran confessed.

He'd done it. He'd bared his soul for the first time since he'd been back. All the shame, all the bottled-up pain… it was now on display for only his wife to see. He was emotionally naked in front of her, and was hoping like crazy that she didn't think it was too much to handle and walk away, even if that's what he secretly expected. When he looked up, he saw his beloved wife trembling, tears coursing down her cheeks.

"My poor Will," she whispered, gently placing her hands on his cheeks. "My poor baby," she sobbed, pulling him to her and kissing him fiercely. "I'm so sorry you had to go through that. I'm so sorry that I've been awful," she buried her face in his chest, as hope and relief flooded through him.

He wrapped his arms around his wife, his cheek resting against the top of her head, drinking in the fresh, clean, familiar scent of her and being, for a moment, transported back in time.

"I love you, baby," he whispered hoarsely, kissing her hair. "I always have."

Rossie leaned back to gaze at him, then traced her fingertip on a scar that ran from his eyebrow to his jawline. "You're still my Will," she murmured, gracing him with the first genuine Rossalyn smile since his return. It was made all the more beautiful by the tears that accompanied it.

Ryan got out of the back seat of his grandmother's car and started toward the house, looking forward to seeing his mom and Barney after a long wonderful vacation in California. The tanned and relaxed teenager came around the corner of the garage and stopped short, his mouth dropping open.

"Dad!" he yelled, charging toward the porch, where Will waited with open arms.

Rossie watched the two of them, her heart over-flowing at the sight. She felt that, at least for now, she'd made the right decision in trying to rebuild her relationship with her husband, and she ignored the twinge of pain that ripped through her when she heard, fading in the distance, the distinct rumble of a motorcycle engine.

***

Did you enjoy this book? Check out book 8 in the series today!

Burnt Endz

ABOUT THE AUTHOR

Summer Prescott is a USA Today and Wall Street Journal Best-Selling Author, who has penned nearly one hundred Cozy Mysteries, and one rather successful Thriller, The Quiet Type, which debuted in the top 50 of its genre. As owner of Summer Prescott Books Publishing, Summer is responsible for a combined catalog of over two hundred Cozy Mysteries and Thrillers. Mentoring and helping new Cozy writers launch their careers has long been a passion of Summer's, and she has played a key role in the incredible success of Cozy writers such as Patti Benning and Carolyn Q. Hunter.

Summer enjoys travel, and is honored to be a featured speaker at the International Writer's Conference in Cuenca, Ecuador, in May 2018. The event draws writers from all over the world.

In an exciting development, Summer has recently been asked to write monthly for her favorite magazine, Atomic Ranch. Having been an Interior Decorator before giving up her business to write full-time, Summer is thrilled by the opportunity and looking forward to having her writing published in the only magazine to which she actually subscribes.

Summer is a doting mother to four grown children, and lives in Champaign, Illinois with her Standard Poodle, Elvis.

AUTHOR'S NOTE

I'd love to hear your thoughts on my books, the story-lines, and anything else that you'd like to comment on —reader feedback is very important to me. My contact information, along with some other helpful links, is listed on the next page. If you'd like to be on my list of "folks to contact" with updates, release and sales notifications, etc.... just shoot me an email and let me know. Thanks for reading!

Also…

… if you're looking for more great reads, Summer Prescott Books publishes several popular series by outstanding Cozy Mystery authors.

CONTACT SUMMER PRESCOTT
BOOKS PUBLISHING

Blog and Book Catalog: http://summerprescottbooks.com

Email: summer.prescott.cozies@gmail.com

And...be sure to check out the Summer Prescott Cozy Mysteries fan page and Summer Prescott Books Publishing Page on Facebook – let's be friends!

Sign up for our fun and exciting newsletter, which will give you opportunities to win prizes and swag, enter contests, and be the first to know about New Releases, click here: http://summerprescottbooks.com